Henry James Pye

Shooting, a Poem

Henry James Pye

Shooting, a Poem

ISBN/EAN: 9783744764018

Printed in Europe, USA, Canada, Australia, Japan

Cover: Foto ©Andreas Hilbeck / pixelio.de

More available books at **www.hansebooks.com**

S H O O T I N G,

A

P O E M.

———— VOLANS LIQUIDIS IN NUBIBUS ARSIT,
SIGNAVITQUE VIAM FLAMMIS ———— ————.

VIRGIL.

L O N D O N:

PRINTED BY J. DAVIS, CHANCERY LANE,
FOR R. FAULDER, NEW BOND STREET, LONDON; AND
MESS. PRINCE AND COOKE, OXFORD.
MDCCLXXXIV.

S H O O T I N G,

A

P O E M.

Y E fylvan mufes! as my ftep invades

The deep receffes of your hallow'd fhades,

Say will ye bid your echoing caves prolong

The harfher cadence of your vot'ry's fong?

Not anxious now to ftrike the trembling wire,   5

Sweetly refponfive to your vernal choir;

Or

Or from the treasur'd stores of earth to bring

The fragrant produce of the roseate spring :

Mine the rude task, while summer's fading ray

To yellow autumn yields the short'ning day,   10

And all the variegated woods appear

Clad in the glories of the withering year,

With dogs and fiery weapons to profane

The peaceful sabbath of your rural reign;

Your desolated regions to explore   15

'Mid the wild tempest, and the season frore ;

Destruction on your feather'd race to pour,

And add new horrors to the wint'ry hour.

   'Twas thine, immortal SOMERVILLE ! to trace

The livelier raptures of the breathless chace,   20

                          O'er

O'er hills and dales to urge, with eager fpeed,

The hound fagacious, and the panting fteed;

And guide the labors of the enthufiaft throng

With all the extatic energy of fong.——

Severer care thefe calmer lays demand,   25

And fancy curb'd by fage Inftruction's hand;

Yet, for the mufe fome fcatter'd charms fhall gleam

'Mid the rich chaos of this copious theme;

Yet, here fhall Glory view, with generous aim,

The rifing elements of martial fame.   30

As from the chace BRITANNIA's youth fhall learn

The docile fteed with ready hand to turn;

O'er the rude crag his bounding fteps to guide,

Or prefs his ardor down the mountain's fide,

Till

Till, rushing to the field with fierce delight, 35

She sends forth other * LINDSEYS to the fight:

So shall the steady train, of careful eye,

Who wound th' aerial offspring as they fly,

Whose limbs unweary'd keep the constant way,

From morn's first opening dawn, till parting day, 40

Manly and firm, an unexhausted race,

With hardy frames the shining phalanx grace;

With steps, by labor unsubdued, shall know

Inceslant to pursue the fainting foe;

Shall, 'midst the rocks and woods, with active toil 45

Hang o'er his march, and all his movements foil;

---

* This gallant Officer, who was killed in one of the descents on the coast of France, during the war before last, was very instrumental in first forming the Light Horse of this country.

Their

Their clofe platoons, with cool and certain aim,

Shall fend deftruction forth in vollied flame ;

Or o'er the field difpers'd, each fhot they pour

Shall mark fome hoftile victim's fatal hour.　　　　　50

Of old, ere imitative mortals ftrove

To mate the fiery bolts of thund'ring Jove,

Train'd by fuperior care, the elaftic yew,

With finewy arm, our Englifh bowmen drew :　　·

The warlike art exulting ALBION faw　　　55

Protected by the foft'ring hand of law;

Attentive * fenates watch'd, with anxious zeal,

This martial bulwark of the general weal ;

* See 33. Hen. VIII ch. 9.

The

The rules they order'd, or the prize they gave,

Compel'd the flothful, and enflam'd the brave ;   60

And oft her archer-fons would trophies wear

From GALLIA's crofsbow won, and SCOTIA's fpear.

   Nor let the frown of literary pride,

Or falfe refinement's fneer, my labors chide :

Not all are form'd with unremitting view   65

Pale ftudy's reftlefs labors to purfue ;

Not all their hours are dull enough to wafte

In the void round of fafhionable tafte ;

Nor can the gentle airings, which engage

The fainter wifh of languor, and of age,   70

From his purfuits the fanguine vot'ry draw

Of wealth, of joy, of wifdom, or of law,

Till

Till flow difeafe demand the leach's care,

Sad fubftitute for exercife and air!

Th' impatient youth, whom manly vigor fires,   75

Ruddy with health, and ftung by wild defires;

By active fports alone can foothe to reft

The boiling fervors of his panting breaft.

Nor fhall BRITANNIA's patriots blame the caufe,

To woods and fields her wealthier chiefs that draws. 80

Let GALLIA's fons to rural fcenes refort

Only when exil'd from a partial court,

Whofe deareft hopes a Monarch's favour crown,

Rais'd by his fmile, or blafted by his frown;

But ALBION's free-er lords muft try to gain   85

The unbiafs'd fuffrage of her ruftic train.

And every tie that binds her nobler band,

With dearer love, to their paternal land,

Her

[8]

Her yeomen fhall behold with grateful eye,

A furer pledge of wealth and liberty.   90

    Come then, ye hardy youths, who wifh to fave

By generous labor powers that nature gave!

Who fly from languor, hufh'd in dread repofe

Beneath the leaves of floth's enchanting rofe,

Glad on the upland brow, or echoing vale,   95

To drink new vigor from the morning gale ;

Come ! and the mufe fhall fhew you how to foil

By fports of fkill the tedious hours of toil;

The healthful leffons of the field impart,

And careful teach the rudiments of art.   100

    When the laft fun of Auguft's fiery reign

Now bathes his radiant forehead in the main,

                                   The

[9]

The panoply by fportive heroes worn

Is ranged in order for the enfuing morn;

Forth from the fummer guard of bolt and lock   105

Comes the thick guêtre, and the fuftian frock;

With curious fkill, the deathful tube is made

Clean as the firelock of the fpruce parade:

Yet, let no polifh of the fportfman's gun

Flafh like the foldier's weapon to the fun,   110

Or the bright fteel's refulgent glare prefume

To penetrate the peaceful foreft's gloom;

But let it take the brown's more fober hue,

Or the dark luftre of the enamel'd blue.

Let the clofe pouch the wadded tow contain,   115

The leaden pellets, and the nitrous grain;

And wifely cautious, with preventive care,

Be the fpare flint, and ready turnfcrew there;

c   While

While the flung net is open to receive

Each prize the labors of the day fhall give.   /120

Yet oft the experienc'd fhooter will deride

This quaint exactnefs of faftidious pride;

In fome old coat that whilom charm'd the eye,

Till time had worn it into flovenry,

His dufky weapon, all by ruft conceal'd,   125

Thro' rainy fervice in the fportive field,

He iffues to the plain, fecure to kill,

And founds his glory on fuperior fkill.

The night recedes, and mild AURORA now

Waves her gray banner on the eaftern brow;   130

Light float the mifty vapours o'er the fky,

And dim the blaze of PHOEBUS' garifh eye;

The

The flitting breeze juft ftirs the ruftling brake,

And curls the cryftal furface of the lake;

Th' expectant fportfmen, urg'd by anxious hafte,   135

Snatch the refrefhment of a fhort repaft,

Their weapons feize, their pointers call around,

And fally forth impatient to the ground.

Here where the yellow wheat away is drawn,

And the thick ftubble clothes the ruffet lawn,   140

Begin the fport.—Eager and unconfin'd

As when ftern ÆOLUS unchains the wind,

The active pointer, from his thong unbound,

Impatient dafhes o'er the dewy ground,

With glowing eye, and undulating tail,   145

Ranges the field, and fnuffs the tainted gale;

           Yet

Yet, midſt his ardor, ſtill his maſter fears,

And the reſtraining whiſtle careful hears.

So when BRITANNIA's watchful navies ſweep,

In freedom's aweful cauſe, the hoſtile deep,   150

Tho' the brave warrior panting to engage,

And looſe on ENGLAND's foes his patriot rage,

The tempeſt's howling fury deems too ſlow

To fill his ſails, and waft him to the foe;

Yet, 'midſt the fiery conflict, if he ſpy   155

From the high maſt his leader's ſignal fly,

To the command obedience inſtant pays,

And martial order martial courage ſways.

See how exact they try the ſtubble o'er,

Quarter the field, and every turn explore;   160

Now

Now fudden wheel, and now attentive feize

The known advantage of th' oppofing breeze.——

At once they ftop!——yon' careful dog defcries

Where clofe and near the lurking covey lies.

His caution mark, left even a breath betray   165

Th' impending danger to his timid prey;

In various attitudes around him ftand,

Silent and motionlefs, the attending band.

So when the fon of DANAE and JOVE,

Crown'd by gay conqueft and fuccefsful love,   170

Saw PHINEUS and his frantic rout invade

The feftive rights by HYMEN facred made,

To the rude Bacchanals his arm outfpread

The horrid image of MEDUSA's head;

Soon as the locks their fnaky curls difclofe,   175

A marble ftiffnefs feiz'd his threat'ning foes;

Fix'd

Fix'd were the eyes that mark'd the javelin thrown,

And each ftern warrior rear'd his lance in ftone.

Now by the glowing cheek and heaving breaft

Is expectation's fanguine wifh exprefs'd.—   180

Ah curb your headlong ardor ! nor refufe

Patient to hear the precepts of the Mufe.

Sooner fhall noify heat in rafh difpute

The reafoning calm of placid fenfe confute·

Sooner the headlong rout's mifguided rage   185

With the firm phalanx equal combat wage,

Than the warm youth, whom anxious hopes enflame,

Purfue the fleeting mark with fteady aim.

By temp'rate thought your glowing paffions cool,

And bow the fwelling heart to reafon's rule ;   190

Elfe

Elfe when the whirring pinion, as it flies,

Alarms your ftartled ear, and dazzled eyes,

Unguided by the cautious arm of care,

Your random bolts fhall wafte their force in air.

They rife !—they rife !—Ah yet your fire reftrain, 195

Till the 'maz'd birds fecurer diftance gain;

For, thrown too clofe, the fhots your hopes elude,

Wide of your aim, and innocent of blood;

But mark with careful eye their leffening flight,

Your ready gun, obedient to your fight,   200

And at the length where frequent trials fhew

Your fatal weapon gives the fureft blow,

Draw quick !—yet fteady care with quicknefs join,

Left the fhock'd barrel deviate from the line;

So

So shall success your ardent wishes pay,　　　　　205

And sure destruction wait the flying prey.

As glory more than gain allures the brave

To dare the combat loud, and louder wave;

So the ambition of the sportsman lies

More in the certain shot than bleeding prize.　　210

While poachers, mindful of the festal hour,

Among the covey random slaughter pour;

And, as their numbers press the crimson'd ground,

Regardless reck not of the secret wound,

Which borne away, the wretched victim's lie　　215

'Mid silent shades to languish and to die.

O let your breast such selfish views disclaim,

And scorn the triumph of a casual aim:

Not

Not urg'd by rapine, but of honor proud,

One object single from the scatt'ring croud;   220

So, when you see the destin'd quarry down,

Shall just applause your skilful labor crown.

    If your staunch dogs require no instant toil

To rescue from their jaws the flutt'ring spoil,

Re-load your fatal piece, with prudent zeal,   225

While glows with recent flame the smoaking steel;

So the black grain shall kindling warmth acquire,

And take the flinty spark with readier fire:

Or if some scatter'd bird, that lay behind,

Sudden should rise, and fleet away on wind,   230

You check her rapid course, nor murm'ring stand,

Your empty weapon useless in your hand.

Now

Now some obfervant eye has mark'd their flight,

And feen difpers'd the weary'd covey light;

Soon to the fpot the ranging pointer drawn,   235

Explores with tender nofe the tainted lawn,

Where, to his nicer fenfe, their fumes betray

The fecret ambufh of the fearful prey.

With cautious action now, and ftealthful pace,

His careful fteps purfue the running race;   240

Now fix'd he ftands, now moves with doubtful tread,

Stop'd by their paufe, or by their motion led,

Till, rooted by the fhelt'ring hedge, his feet

Declare the trembling victim's laft retreat.

But as, with beating breafts, on either fide   245

Th' impatient youths the pleafing tafk divide,

And

And in the row between the lurking game

Lies hid from fight, ah, careful be the aim !

Left, fkreen'd and parted by the thorny mound,

The erring fhots fhould give a fatal wound,　　250

And change the jocund fportfman's verdant wreath

For fun'ral weeds, for mourning, tears, and death.

In LYDIAN plains, where rich PACTOLUS roll'd

Through groves of perfume, and o'er fands of gold,

CROESUS, of ASIA's lords the proudeft name,　　255

Shar'd every gift of fortune, and of fame ;

So wide his empire, and fo vaft his ftore,

That av'rice and ambition afk'd no more ;

Tho' bleft in thefe, the dearer blifs he knows

With which a parent's happy bofom glows,　　260

　　　　　　For

For not the faireft image ever drefs'd

In the fond wifhes of a father's breaft,

By flattery fwell'd, could mate the virtuous praife

To ATYS' worth that truth unbiafs'd pays.

At war's loud clarion if the nations bled,   . 265

Conqueft his armies crown'd if ATYS led;

If the rude waves of civil difcord broke,

Hufh'd was the rifing ftorm if ATYS fpoke;

His lenient voice bade loud rebellion ceafe,

And charm'd contending factions into peace :   270

Nor lefs his care domeftic knew to bring

Joy to his fire, than fafety to his king ;

Nor was the patriot's glory priz'd above

The dearer charity of filial love.

While

While profp'rous fcenes the monarch's thoughts beguile,

Too little warn'd of Fortune's tranfient fmile,

'Mid the dark moments of the boding night

A horrid vifion feem'd to meet his fight,

With dying mien his ATYS ftood confefs'd,

Transfix'd by hoftile fteel his bleeding breaft.—— 280

Swift from his couch he ftarts, while wild defpair

Contracts his eyeballs, and uplifts his hair.

In vain the orient morn's reviving pow'r

Chaced the pale phantoms of the midnight hour;

The recollected fcene his peace annoys, 285

Sinks in his heart, and poifons all his joys;

Around him vifionary falchions gleam

In act to realize his dreadful dream;

And if by chance loud rumour wafts from far

Uncertain clamours of intended war, 290

His

His lab'ring breaft foretells the fatal deed,

And fees in fancied fights his ATYS bleed.

What fhall his fears invent, or how controul

The generous ardor of the hero's foul ?——

. His mind to gentler thoughts he tries to move,   295

And conquer ftrong renown by ftronger love

The faireft maid of LYDIA's glowing dames,

Whofe beauteous form the manly youth enflames,

With eaftern rofes crown'd, is blufhing led

In Hymeneal pomp, to ATYS' bed.   300

To cares of empire, and to toils of fight,

Succeed the feftal day, and genial night;

Soft Pleafure fpreads around her blooming flow'rs,

And wanton CUPID leads the laughing hours.

Thro' fragrant myrtle groves amaranthine flowers

addenda incerti authoris.

Amid

Amid thefe joys, from MYSIA's fubject plain,   305

Before the throne, behold a fuppliant train !

" O mighty prince !" they cry, " we now repair

" To claim the aid of thy paternal care;

" A favage monfter of portentous fize,

" Whofe cruel ftrength our utmoft force defies,   310

" Ranges our fields, fpreads devaftation round,

" And roots th' unripen'd harveft from the ground.

" O, let thy youths, to range the woods who know,

" Attend with faithful dogs, and twanging bow ;

" In his dire haunts the fierce invader brave,   315

" Repel his fury, and thy fubjects fave.

" Perhaps the prince."------The eager monarch, here,

Urg'd by the influence of parental fear,

Arrefts their fpeech: " My arms, my youths fhall go,

" Your terrors quell, and check this favage foe ;   320

                                                              " But

" But for my fon, him other cares employ,

" And the foft fcenes of Hymeneal joy,

" Nor muft the rugged chace, or dubious fight,

" Mar the fweet tranfports of the nuptial rite."

He ceas'd ; attentive round the MYSIAN band,　　325

Pleas'd with the promis'd aid, fubmiffive ftand.

Not fo the prince, his ardent bofom glows

To burft the filken bands of ftill repofe.

" Ah ! what, my fire," he cries, " has ATYS done ?

" What fad diftruft awaits your haplefs fon,　　330

" That thus immers'd in floth you keep him far

" From fields of glory, and from toils of war ?

" For love's foft raptures though the hero burn,

" Yet fame and danger claim their wonted turn.

How

[25]

" How fhall I meet, involv'd in this difgrace,   335

" The indignant murmurs of your warrior race?

" How will, with tears of filent fcorn, my bride

" Her alter'd lord's inglorious fafety chide!

" O give my wifhes way, or let me hear

" The hidden fource of this injurious fear."   340

This earneft prayer the fmother'd fecret draws,

And the fad Monarch owns the latent caufe:

When ATYS, fmiling:—" How fhall I reprove

" The fond exceffes of paternal love,

" Tho' for my undeferving life is fhown   345

" A nice regard you never paid your own?

" But fhall the heir of CROESUS' martial name

" Inglorious life prefer to glorious fame?——

E   " Life

" Life is a blifs, when crown'd by virtue's meed,

" And death a prize, when honor bids us bleed ; 350

" Omens and dreams in vain the purpofe ftay

" When duty calls, and glory points the way.

" Or grant fome god the vifion fent, yet here

" Vain are your cares, and ufelefs is your fear ;

" Tranfix'd by fteel my bleeding breaft you faw, 355

" Not torn and mangled by a beftial jaw ;

" Then let me go, and when you meet your fon

" Clad in the fhaggy fpoils his arms have won,

" The fhadowy phantoms of the night fhall ceafe

" To haunt your flumbers, and difturb your peace." 360

The Monarch hears, and with reluctant eyes

Gives the confent his boding heart denies ;

His

His brow a placid guife diffembling wears,

While reafon vainly combats ftronger fears.

It chanc'd a youth of PHRYGIA's royal train,   365

His hand polluted by a brother flain,

Exil'd by vengeance from his native ground,

In CROESUS' peaceful court a refuge found ;

Where oft would ATYS' gentler care impart

The balm of friendfhip to his wounded heart ;   370

To him the wretched king in fecret fpoke,

While tears and fighs his faltering accents choke;

" If, brave ADRASTUS, thy oppreffive woes

" In SARDIS' fheltering walls have found repofe,

" If here the expiating rite renew'd   375

" Has paid the forfeit for fraternal blood,

       " If

[28]

"If pity's tear, if friendship's lenient balm

"Have tried with studious zeal thy griefs to calm,

"Go with my son, and by attentive care

"Partake his labors, and his dangers share.   380

"Shield him from peril that my soul alarms,

"And bring him back in safety to my arms."

To whom the youth : "Oft has my ready breast

"Panted to ask the office you request,

"As oft my conscious shame that wish restrain'd,   385

"Disgrac'd by exile, and by murder stain'd :

"Since you command, your ATYS I'll attend,

"Obey my patron, and protect my friend;

"Watch o'er his safety in the doubtful strife,

"Or ransom with my own his dearer life."   390

Now

Now to the Myfian fields elate and gay

The eager warriors bend their jocund way, *a road personified*

The echoing hills and foreft walks refound

With fhouts of men, and chidings of the hound. *only one*

Rous'd from his lair, and iffuing on the plain,   395

Forth burfts the monfter on the hunter train,

Around the circling youths impatient ftand,

And launch their fteely darts with ready hand. *or steelclad*

Too rafhly eager as the PHRYGIAN threw,

With erring aim the pointed jav'lin flew,   400

In ATYS' breaft the quiv'ring weapon ftood, *I now an arrow her*

And drank with fatal barbs his vital blood.—

The mournful fhrieks that rent the ambient air,

The weeping troops, ADRASTUS' loud defpair;

The filent agony, the gufhing tide   405

Of the fad parent, and the widow'd bride,

      The

The plaints they utter, and the woes they feel,

No heart can image, and no tongue reveal.

As the ill-fated youth is borne along,

All pale and bleeding, thro' the groaning throng,   410

By the cold corfe ADRASTUS frantic cries,

Death in his voice, and horror in his eyes;

" Why have the gods in partial vengeance fhed

" Their choiceft curfes on my wretched head?

" Fated the keeneft ftrokes of wrath to prove,   415

" And doom'd to murder thofe whom moft I love!

" O much wrong'd fire, let thy avenging hand

" Expiate by guilty blood this weeping land:

" Be on my heart thy inftant fury hurl'd,

" And fave from future paricide the world!   420

" Alas

" Alas, my fon !" the wretched King replied,

" 'Tis aweful JOVE who thus corrects my pride,

" Which, crown'd by conqueft, and with power elate,

" Its fortune deem'd beyond the reach of fate.

" Alas ! too late repentant, now I find   425

" The fleeting happinefs of human kind !

" With unexpected fhock, this cruel blow

" Has laid at once my vain ambition low;

" The offended gods this chaftifement have given,

" Thou but the fatal inftrument of heaven."   430

Silent the youth withdrew, till fad were paid

The tributary rites to ATYS' fhade :

Then, as chill midnight's dreary hours return,

Weeping he fought the monumental urn :——

                                " ATYS !"

" ATYS !" he cried, " behold ADRASTUS come   435

" A willing victim to thy hallow'd tomb !—

" This erring hand, the fatal ftroke that gave,

" Shall lay thy murderer breathlefs on thy grave."

Then pierc'd with fudden arm his ftruggling breaft,

And on the blood-ftain'd marble funk to reft.   440

As more obliquely on autumnal fkies

With milder force October's funs arife,

The purple pheafant tempts the youth to rove

With well train'd fpaniels thro' the faded grove.

See how with emulative zeal they ftrive,   445

Thrid the loofe fedge, and thro' the thicket drive !

Not ranging lawlefs o'er the foreft wide,

But clofe attendant on their mafter's fide ;

No

No babbling voice the bosom falsely warms,

Or swells the panting heart with vain alarms,   450

Till all at once their choral tongues proclaim

The secret refuge of the lurking game;

Loud on the breeze the chearful clamour floats,

And the high wood re-echoes with the notes.

Swift is their course, no lengthen'd warnings now   455

Space to collect the scatter'd thoughts allow,

No wary pointer shews the cautious eyes

Where from his russet couch the bird shall rise:

Perhaps light running o'er the mossy ground,

His devious steps your sanguine hopes confound;   460

Or, by the tangled branches hid from sight,

Sudden he wings his unexpected flight.

No open view along the uncumber'd field

To the cool aim will time and distance yield;

F   But

But the nice circumſtance will oft demand   465

The quickeſt eyeſight, and the readieſt hand,

Swift as he riſes from the thorny brake,

With inſtant glance the fleeting mark to take,

And with prompt arm the tranſient moment ſeize,

'Mid the dim gloom of intervening trees.   470

His gaudy plumage when the male diſplays

In bright luxuriance to the ſolar rays,

Arreſt with haſty ſhot his whirring ſpeed,

And ſee unblamed the ſhining victim bleed ;

But when the hen to thy diſcerning view   475

Her ſober pinion ſpreads of duſkier hue,

The attendant keeper's prudent warning hear,

And ſpare the offspring of the future year,

Elſe ſhall the fine which cuſtom laid of old

Avenge her ſlaughter by thy forfeit gold.   480

Soon

Soon as the ready dogs their quarry spring,

And swift he spreads his variegated wing,

Ceased is their cry, with silent look they wait

Till the loud gun decides the event of fate;

Nor, if the shots are thrown with erring aim,   485

And proudly soars away the unwounded game,

Will the staunch train pursue him as he flies

With useless speed, and unavailing cries.

And now when cloudy skies and drizzly rains

Swell the full springs, and drench the moisten'd plains, 490

The extended space of land and ocean cross'd

From the bleak scenes of Hyperborean frost,

With active wing the unwearied Woodcocks fly

To southern climates, and a milder sky,

The

The ozier'd borders of the brook explore,   495

And with deep bills the foreft marfhes bore. *twaddle*

Where now matured yon flender afhes ftand,

Rife from their ftools and tempt the woodman's hand,

Where the loofe trunks admit the partial ray

Along the border take your cautious way.   500

Here let your care the fhorten'd gun employ,

Left the thick boughs the purpofed aim annoy;

Let fuper-added fteel with preffure fure,

From the dank drip the fhelter'd pan fecure:

And as the filent bird the ftems among   505

Wheels flow his defultory flight along,

With fteady eye his wavering motion watch,

And thro' the parting trees the advantage catch;

Tho' diftant be the fhot, the flighteft wound

Shall lay the fluttering victim on the ground.   510

                                      Roufed

Roufed by the fpaniel, 'midft the foreft fhade,

Behold the trembling Leveret crofs the glade !

If round the extended plains yield ample fpace,

Or for the rapid courfe, or chearful chace,

O, facred be her fteps ! nor let thy hand   515

Blaft the fair hopes of a congenial band,

Or for a tranfient pleafure meanly foil

The lengthen'd tranfport of the hunter's toil;

But where fteep hills and fpacious woodlands rife,

Or the long flight the frequent copfe denies,   520

Blamelefs arreft her rapid flight, nor fpare

The timid victim for the inglorious fnare.

Where fhining rills with copious moifture feed

The deeper verdure of the irriguous mead,

Or

Or where between the purple heaths is seen   525

The mossy bosom of the low ravine,

The fearful Snipes, hid from the searching eye,

'Mid the dank sedge and nodding rushes lie.

With sudden turns oblique, when first they rise,

As from the weaver's arm the shuttle flies   530

They shape their wavering course; but patient stay

Till, with securer wing, they soar away;

Then as aloft their outstretch'd pinions sail,

Borne on the bosom of the buoyant gale;

The fatal shot sent forth with cautious sight,   535

Shall bring them wheeling from their towering height.

When winter now, a gloomy tyrant, reigns

In dreadful silence o'er the ravaged plains,

                                     Involves

[39]

Involves in sheets of snow the bending woods,

And throws his icy mantle o'er the floods,   540

Close by the harden'd brook, whose sullen stream

No more soft murmuring aids the poet's dream,

Where, 'midst the matted sedge, the emerging flood

With air and life renews the finny brood,

The patient fowler stands with silent aim   545

To watch the station of the watery game:

Not like the gentle angler, careless laid

In the cool shelter of the summer shade,

But train'd with hardy sinews to defy

The chilling keenness of a wintery sky;   550

While here the aquatic Wild-fowl's timid race

With wonted pinion seek the well known place;

Where rushes thick the Widgeon's haunt conceal,

The blue-winged Mallard, and the tenderer Teal;

Swift

[40]

Swift on the various race, in fiery fhower,   555

The fcattering fhots unfeen deftruction pour,

With mingled flaughter ftrew the froft-bound flood,

And dye the fullied fnow with gufhing blood.

Such are the fports that fertile ALBION yields,

Such the wing'd inmates of her milder fields ;   560

But bounteous Nature, with diffufive hand,

Spreads wide her various produce o'er the land,

Each different region marks with nurturing care,

And bids a race congenial flourifh there.

A tribe peculiar by her power is plac'd   565

On the drear mountain, and the howling wafte,

Which art and induftry would rear in vain,

Or in the fheltered vale, or cultured plain.

Hence

[41]

Hence wandering far from ENGLAND's gentler scene,

Her spacious champains, and her pastures green,   570

The hardy youth will CAMBRIA's cliffs explore,

Or climb the heights of CALEDONIA hoar,

The Grouse and sable Heath-cock to pursue

Where moors unbounded tire the sated view,

While noontide silence reigns, save where the tide   575

Pours in swoln torrents from the mountain's side ;

And summer suns in full effulgence shed

Their burning fervors on the throbbing head.

    Thus has my verse in humble strains reveal'd

The various pleasures of the sportive field,   580

And shewn the different labors of the day

As the revolving seasons roll away :

But vainly fhall preceptive rules.impart

A perfect knowledge of this manly art ;

Practice alone can certain fkill produce,   585

And theory confirm'd by conftant ufe.

As well the ftripling of the gay parade,

Proud of his filken fafh and fmart cockade,

Tho' taught by wife inftructors to explore

The martial depth of mathematic lore,   590

Might hope to drive VICTORIA's crimfon car

Triumphant o'er the bleeding ranks of war,

Ere the long march, the early toil, and late,

The frequent fcenes of danger and of fate,

The fervor of the glowing breaft allay,   595

Change ardor's blaze for valor's temperate ray,

And teach the mind, unruffled and ferene,

To keep her powers 'midft horrors wildeft fcene.

The

The hardy youth who pants with eager flame

To fend his leaden bolts with certain aim,   600

Muſt ne'er with difappointed hopes recoil

From cold and heat, from hunger and from toil,

Muſt climb the hill, muſt tread the marſhy glade,

Or force his paſſage thro' the oppoſing ſhade,

Muſt range untamed by SOL's meridian power,   605

And brave the force of winter's keeneſt hour,

Till induſtry and time their work have wrought,

And honor crown the ſkill that labor taught.

Yet ſome, theſe harſher rudiments to ſpare,

And equal art with eaſier toil to ſhare,   610

Or watch with careful aim and ready ſight

The ſwallow wheeling in her ſummer flight,

G 2   Or

Or on fome lofty cliff, whofe chalky fleep

Hangs with rude brow impending o'er the deep,

Where gulls and fcreaming fea-mews haunt the rock, 615

Pour fire inceffant on the mingled flock.

But vain their hopes—prefented to the eye

In fuch diverfive lines the objects fly,

That the 'maz'd fight unnumber'd marks purfues,

Uncertain where to aim, and which to chufe ;   620

Decifion quick and calm, the fhooter's boaft,

By frequent change, is check'd, confus'd, and loft,

And, guarded by irrefolute delay,

Untouch'd fhall future coveys fleet away.

More hurtful ftill to try with diftant blow   625

To bring the percher from th' aerial bough.

How

How fhall his thoughts the level that prepare

With all the caution of mechanic care,

Exact and fteady as the fage's eye

Thro' GALILEO's tube furveys the fky,   630

With ready view the tranfient object feize

Swift as the motion of the rapid breeze,

Purfue the uncertain mark with fwift addrefs,

And catch the fleeting moment of fuccefs ?

　　Ere yet the Mufe her lay preceptive end   635

Ye eager youths thefe friendly rules attend :

'Tis not enough, that cautious aim, and fure,

From erring fhots your brave compeers fecure,

That prudence guard thofe ills which erft might flow

From the wing'd javelin, and the founding bow ;   640

　　　　　　　　　　　　　　　　　　　　　　For

For on the gun unnumber'd dangers wait,

And various forms of unexpected fate.

Drawn thro' the thorny hedge, the uncertain lock

May give with fudden fpring, a deadly fhock ;

Or the loofe fpark the rapid flafh may raife,   645

And wrap the fulphurous duft in inftant blaze.

'Tis hence the military race prepare

The novice youth with fuch affiduous care,

And teach him with punctilious art to wield

The weighty fire-lock in the embattled field.   650

Tho' fome may deem the attention urg'd too far,

As the meer pomp and circumftance of war ;

When clofely wedged the firm battalions ftand,

Rank prefs'd on rank, and band impelling band,

Did

Did not faftidious zeal with cautious plan   655

Define each act, and every motion fcan,

Oft would the bullet 'mid the battles roar

The thirfty herbage die with friendly gore,

And oft the dangerous weapon's kindling breath

Change fields of exercife, to fields of death.   660

    Behold yon' eager race who o'er the plain,

With ftimulating heel and loofen'd reign,

Their panting courfers urge to leave behind

The rapid currents of the northern wind,

Tho', as with headlong rage they rufh along,   665

Impending dangers feem to wait the throng;

Tho' accident with more apparent face

Seem to attend the ardor of the chace;

                                        Yet,

Yet, 'midſt theſe calmer ſports, with ghaſtly mien

The pallid form of ſlaughter lurks unſeen ;   670

And while the hunter checks his bold career

To pour on RUSSEL's tomb the ſorrowing tear,

The ſportive train who haunt the fatal glades

Where hoary CAMUS flows by GRANTA's ſhades,

Shall weep the unexpected blow that gave   675

Their much-loved COTTON to a timeleſs grave.

Lamented youth ! when erſt on WARLEY's plains

We led in radiant arms our ruſtic ſwains,

What time BRITANNIA, friendleſs and forlorn,

Her ſhores expoſed, her naval trophies torn ;   680

Bold in her native vigor dared oppoſe

Rebellious ſubjects, and combining foes ;

In vain thy generous boſom burn'd to ſtand

The manly bulwark of an injured land,

Or

Or nobly bleeding by the hoftile ball,   685

In freedom's, and in ALBION's caufe to fall;

Doom'd by relentlefs fate, to prefs the ground,

The unhappy victim of a cafual wound.

   Votaries of rural joy ! with mine while flow

Your kindred ftreams of fympathetic woe,   690

By falutary care, ah ! learn to fhun

The hidden dangers of the unguarded gun !

And, as in fields of pleafure you acquire

The foldier's manly toil and fteady fire,

His cautious ufe of arms attentive heed,   695

Careful by no inglorious wound to bleed,

Nor lavifh life, but in the facred caufe

Of BRITAIN's injured rights, and violated laws.

T H E   E N D.

764018*